Dorkius Maximus

TIM COLLINS

BUSTER

Written by Tim Collins
Illustrated by Andrew Pinder

Edited by Bryony Jones and Philippa Wingate
Cover designed by Angie Allison
Designed by Barbara Ward

First published in Great Britain in 2013 by Buster Books,
an imprint of Michael O'Mara Books Limited,
9 Lion Yard, Tremadoc Road, London SW4 7NQ

www.busterbooks.co.uk

A CIP catalogue record for this book is available
from the British Library.

ISBN: 978-1-78055-027-5 in paperback print format
ISBN: 978-1-78055-188-3 in Epub format
ISBN: 978-1-78055-189-0 in Mobipocket format

1 3 5 7 9 10 8 6 4 2

Papers used by Michael O'Mara Books are natural,
recyclable products made from wood grown in sustainable forests.
The manufacturing processes conform to the environmental
regulations of the country of origin.

Printed and bound in January 2013 by CPI Group (UK) Ltd,
108 Beddington Lane, Croydon, CR0 4YY, United Kingdom.

Acknowledgements

Thanks to Bryony Jones, Philippa Wingate,
John Malam, Hilary Larkin,
Andrew Pinder and Collette Collins.

Mum and Dad

My so-called friends,
Cornelius, Gaius and Flavia

Brawnus, the
brother I'll never
live up to

Brilliant
(and balding)
Julius Caesar

Mum's sacred
pigs and chickens

THIS DIARY BELONGS
TO: DORKIUS MAXIMUS
AGED: 12 YEARS
ALMOST a Roman hero

Linos, Greek slave
boy and my future
best friend (if Dad
would buy him)

Brilliant tutor,
Stoutus

Mum's doctor,
Vibius

BORING
tutor, Lucius

March 1

Dad gave me this papyrus scroll today. I'm going to use it to jot down the things that happen to me every day. Then when I'm a noble Roman hero, I'll have a complete record of how I rose to greatness.

Future Dorkius Maximus, awesome Roman hero

I need to work on the noble hero thing, though. Last time I tried on my brother Brawnus's hand-me-down armour I fell over backwards. It was TOTALLY embarrassing. How am I supposed to strike fear into the hearts of the enemy when I can't even stand up?

HA HA HA!

Surrender!

But I know I'm destined for big things. After all, Dad used to be in the army and now he's gone into politics. Brawnus is just a few years older than me, and he's already a general. So I bet there's a mighty warrior inside me waiting to get out.

I just hope he turns up soon.

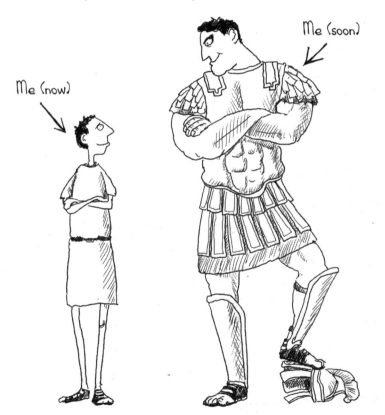

Me (soon)

Me (now)

March 11

I got kicked out of the kitchen today for stealing a dormouse.

The slaves were frantically preparing goose livers, cows' udders and dormice in honey for a dinner party tonight. I didn't think they'd miss a roast mouse, but one of them smacked it out of my hand and told me to wait until later.

I HATE dinner parties. The food might be tasty but the guests are disgusting. They always spew into buckets so they can cram in more food.

It's so gross. Just the sound of their retching is enough to make me want to barf too. And throwing up is like yawning. As soon as someone does it, you can't help but join in.

I wish they'd let me take my food back to my room, but Dad says this is 'anti-social'. And spraying our dining room with vomit isn't?

I can't sleep because the party is so noisy. I just heard a massive cheer from the garden and peeked outside. Dad's hired a couple of dwarfs to dress up as gladiators and fight each other.*

If I go and ask them to keep the noise down, Dad will only make me join in. Then I'll get stabbed to death by a miniature trident, which will leave me with a lot of explaining to do in the afterlife.

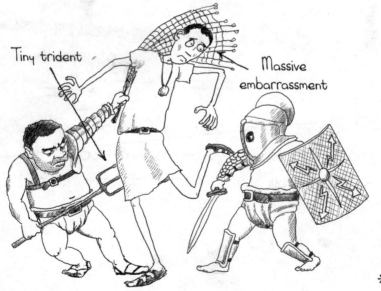

Tiny trident

Massive embarrassment

* Tricky Roman words are explained at the back.

I've been worrying about the afterlife a lot recently.

Mum says when you die, you have to take a ferry across the River Styx and give an account of your life to three judges. If you've been bad, they send you to a nasty place called Tartarus, which is even more horrible than having a maths lesson and going to the dentist at the same time.

If you've been good, they send you to somewhere boring called the Plain of Asphodel. But if you've been completely brilliant they send you to the sunny fields of Elysium.

When I die I want to hang out with the heroes of Elysium, not the sad-acts of Asphodel or the losers of Tartarus.

But how will I get in if I die from falling downstairs in armour or getting stabbed by a tiny trident?

I need to become a noble Roman hero RIGHT NOW ... I can't wait any longer.

March III

I just asked Dad if he would train me to be a mighty hero. He said I should wait until I grow a bit taller, as it would be a waste of time at the moment.

I'm sick of waiting to grow. Brawnus was much taller than me when he was my age. Maybe this is as tall as I'm going to get.

I followed Dad around all morning, pestering him to train me. Eventually, he gave in and handed me one of his swords.

I tried to let out a roar like a mighty warrior, but I sent myself into a coughing fit and had to drink some water.

When I'd recovered, Dad took me out into
the atrium and tied a sack of grain to one
of the pillars.

'Imagine that's a barbarian running towards
you in battle,' said Dad. 'In real life the
barbarian would smell of goats and have a
long, straggly beard — especially if he was a
she. But the sack will have to do for now.'

I lifted the sword over my head, ready
to bring it down with all my strength.
Unfortunately, it was much heavier than I'd
realized, and I fell over backwards ... again.

I heard laughter from the other side of the
atrium and saw all the servants watching.

'Silence,' shouted Dad. 'My son will try
again and no one will laugh.'

I lifted the sword again and tried swinging it round to the side, missed the grain sack and carried on going until I hit something else. Unfortunately, the something else turned out to be Mum's favourite vase. It wobbled one way, then the other, then fell to the floor and shattered.

Uh-oh. Dad was right. Nobody laughed this time. They were all too busy shaking their heads and wincing.

Bloodthirsty barbarian – hit this.

Expensive vase – don't hit this.

March IV

I went down to the forum with Dad today to buy some more ink, but when we got there, I was desperate for the loo.

Dad wouldn't let me go back home and made me use the public toilet. I HATE public toilets. I sat down next to three men who were discussing something boring, while farting so loudly it sounded like their bottoms were having a separate conversation.

I really can't go with other people sitting next to me. In the end, after trying to go for ages, I gave up. I faked a look of relief and stood up. The man next to me turned round and said, 'Don't be disgusting.'

ME disgusting! He sounded like he was squeezing a cowpat out of his backside. How could he possibly find ME disgusting?

'You haven't wiped,' he said, handing me a sponge on a stick. Oops – I'd forgotten about that. But who wants to wipe with a sponge that loads of other people have used first?

I pretended to use the stick and handed it back. How will I ever become a noble hero if I don't even have the courage to take a dump in public?

Wiping end

DON'T get these mixed up.

Holding end

March V

Mum heard some thunder last night and thought it was a bad omen about Brawnus. As usual, she overreacted — she bought a pig, and got her priest to kill it and read its innards in the temple.

Guess what the innards said? Brawnus will be fine. Even if they hadn't, what could we have done about it anyway, with him so far away fighting with the army? Absolutely nothing. What a waste of a pig.

I wish those innards could predict something useful, like who's going to win the chariot race next week. Then we could win back some of the money Mum keeps spending on pigs.

March VI

I spotted Mum's priest in the forum this morning, looking suspicious and lugging a heavy sack. I followed him to see what he was up to.

He headed to the butcher's stall, glanced over his shoulder, untied the sack and handed over the remains of a pig.

The butcher examined it, nodded and gave him four coins.

So THAT'S why the priest is so keen on killing pigs. Well, he can't be that brilliant at telling the future, or he'd have chosen a time when no one would be watching.

I told Dad about the priest's scam and he went nuts. Then he told Mum she had to change priests, and she freaked out, too.

'The gods will punish us,' she wailed.

'The gods have already cursed me with a batty wife and a disappointing son,' said Dad. 'What more could they do to me?'

Disappointing? What a strange thing to say about Brawnus.

Later on, Dad started feeling guilty about shouting, so he bought Mum some sacred chickens to make it up to her. Now she can augur from home. Apparently, all she has to do is offer seed cake to the chickens. If they eat the cake, it's a good omen. If they refuse, it's a bad one.

I'm not quite sure what the logic behind all this is, but if it cuts down on the number of pigs Mum gets through, I'm all for it.

Sacred chicken   Normal chicken

March VII

Today I asked Dad if I could have another hero lesson, but he refused.

'Everyone has different skills,' he said. 'Some people, like your brother Brawnus, are meant to be mighty heroes. Others are meant for less ... physically demanding things.'

'Like what?' I asked.

'You could be a food-taster,' he said. 'That's a great job. You get to sit around all day testing food for rich people. And they always need new tasters, as the old ones keep dying of poisoning.'

'No,' I said. 'NOT interested.'

'Well, you could ask Mum's friend Vibius how to become a doctor,' said Dad. 'He's one, and he's had absolutely no training at all. Or you could be a professional armpit-plucker. I met one in the baths the other day. He says it's good work if you can put up with the smell. AND they let you keep the hairs.'

'I don't want to be an armpit-plucker,'
I said. 'I don't want to be any of those
boring things. I want to be a mighty Roman
hero and I demand that you train me
right away.'

Unfortunately, Dad just turned around and
walked away.

March VIII

We were supposed to go to the forum today so I could buy a new scroll. But Mum wouldn't let me go because her stupid chickens wouldn't eat their cake.

I don't want to question Mum's crackpot beliefs, but maybe the chickens just weren't hungry?

She didn't seem to like it when I suggested that to her, so I'll just have to end my diary here because I've run out of space. I just hope nothing interesting happens today, because I won't be able to write about it ...

March IX

The chickens ate their cake this morning, so I was allowed to go out and buy this new scroll.

The stall-keeper asked what I thought about the elephants. WHAT elephants?

Apparently four elephants were marched through the streets yesterday afternoon. There's going to be a huge parade next month in honour of Julius Caesar, and the animals have been brought over from Africa for it.

I can't believe I missed them. I've ALWAYS wanted to see an elephant. Cornelius says they're as big as carriages and have a tail at the front as well as the back.

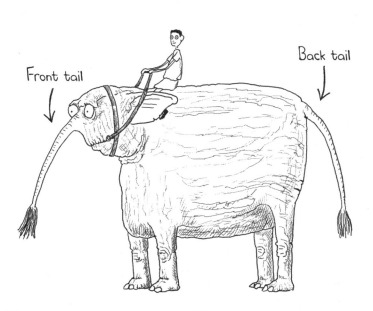

Front tail

Back tail

Thanks a lot, chickens. Thanks for stopping me seeing something totally brilliant. What will you save me from next? Someone giving out free money?

Well, let me tell you dumb birds something. If you dare try and make me miss the parade next month, you're going straight into the cooking pot. I don't care if you're sacred chickens. You'll be sacred chickens in asparagus sauce with onions if you don't stop meddling in my life.

March X

Mum took my tunic to the laundry today and it came back smelling of wee. When I complained, she said it wasn't surprising, as wee is exactly what they wash it in. GROSS!

Apparently, the laundry workers leave buckets on street corners for people to wee in. Obviously, you'd never catch me doing that, not the way I feel about going to the loo in public.

The full buckets are taken to the laundry, and the wee is mixed with water in giant tubs.

Slaves stamp on the clothes to clean them.

Stink

Water

Wee

Imagine doing that on a really hot day. It's making my eyes water just thinking about it.

I told Mum I'd rather have a dirty tunic that didn't smell of wee, but she didn't take any notice. I bet if I weed on things to wash them, she'd freak out. But when the slaves do it, it's a different story.

Hang on, I'm just cleaning my room.

March XI

My tutor Lucius came round to give me another boring, boring, boring maths lesson. Did I mention that it was boring?

I won't need to know maths when I'm a mighty hero. The only thing I'll need to add up is the number of smelly barbarians I've killed. AND I'll get a slave to do that for me.

March XII

Tomorrow we're going to the amphitheatre to watch my favourite gladiator Triumphus fight, and I can't wait. I LOVE Triumphus. He has a trident, a net and armour down his left arm. He's so tough he doesn't even wear a mask.

38

For my last birthday, I was actually given what I wanted, for once. I got a brilliant mosaic of him on my bedroom floor.

You should have seen how jealous my friends Cornelius and Gaius were when they saw it. Neither of them would ever be allowed anything so amazing.

March XIII

Today I went to see Triumphus fight against a new gladiator called Flamma.

I thought Triumphus would cruise to victory as usual, but Flamma was really strong and wouldn't give up.

After half an hour, Triumphus collapsed on to the sand and Flamma stood over him, clutching his dagger.

The crowd in the amphitheatre started to chant, 'Kill him! Kill him!'

I tried to start a rival chant of 'Let him go!' Nobody joined in. In fact, the man in front of me told me to shut up.

You're spoiling my fun!

Never mind your fun. What about my mosaic?

The roaring of the crowd got louder and louder, until Flamma thrust his dagger into Triumphus's heart, turning the sand red.

The crowd went crazy, but I was gutted. My mosaic is TOTALLY out of date now.

March XIV

I just asked Dad if he'd replace my
Triumphus mosaic with one of Flamma, but
he refused. I can't believe how stingy he is.
When you think how much money Mum has
wasted on pigs, it's ridiculous that he won't
pay for something as important as this.

This afternoon I tried on Brawnus's old tunic
and it still went down to below my knees. I
thought I'd grown since last time I tried it
on, but I must have been imagining it.

I'm going to pray to the gods right now to
make me as big and strong as my brother.

Well, that didn't work. I'm still the same size. I'm not sure I prayed very well, though. I didn't have an animal to offer so I thought a cabbage would have to do.

Mum rushed in and told me off for wasting perfectly good food. That was so hypocritical I don't know where to start.

March XV

Things are looking up at long, long last. Today's the Ides of March, the day of the year we're supposed to celebrate Mars, the god of war.

I did my bit by running into my parents' room, swinging Dad's sword around and shouting, 'I am a mighty warrior.'

Dad leapt up and shielded the vase next to his bed. 'Put that down, Dorkius,' he shouted. 'I'll give you whatever you want. Just put the sword down.'

'Whatever I want?' I asked. 'Alright then. Train me to be a noble hero.'

When Dad came home this evening, he said he'd asked his old army friend Stoutus to train me in the art of combat.

I'm going to meet Stoutus tomorrow. If he agrees to take me on, he'll replace dull old Lucius as my tutor. I really hope he wants to teach me. Just imagine how tough I'll be with all that training. I'll be able to wipe out whole tribes of barbarians with a single slash of my sword.

Mum reckons her chickens have warned that my combat training will end in tragedy. No, they haven't. They just weren't hungry … again.

Dad said that the chickens might be right, but if he lets me train here, there will definitely be a tragedy. The entire villa, including the sacred chickens themselves, will be hacked to shreds.

This is clearly nonsense, but I didn't argue.
Anything to get my training.

March XVI

Stoutus lives in a large house on top of Quirinal Hill. When I got there, one of his servants led me through to the large walled garden at the back.

The first thing I saw was a huge statue of Stoutus. It was tall, rippling with muscles and holding a sword.

Then the real Stoutus stepped out from behind it. He was short, fat and munching on a chicken leg.

I wondered if Stoutus would be fit enough to train me, but then he dragged the heavy statue over to the edge of the garden with one hand. It looks like he still has the strength of a mighty warrior, even if he doesn't look like one.

Stoutus handed me a wooden sword. 'Show me what you can do, boy.'

Stoutus: mighty hero

Stoutus: mighty appetite

STOUTUS

I grabbed the sword with both hands and spun round and round. Stoutus seemed pretty unimpressed. He tossed the chicken bone over his shoulder and scowled.

I wondered what I could do to convince
him. I closed my eyes and pretended I was
Triumphus. Back when he was alive, I mean.
I DIDN'T pretend to be a dead gladiator.

I mimed all Triumphus's best moves, gripping
the sword with my right hand and attacking
in short, quick jabs.

Stoutus walked over, pulled my shoulders
back and pushed my chin up. His hands were
really greasy from the chicken.

'Imagine the sword is part of your arm,'
he said.

This made me imagine a man with one really
short arm and one long arm, and I had to
stop myself sniggering. I took a deep breath,
thought about Triumphus again, and tried a
few more attack moves.

'Okay,' he said finally. 'Tell your Dad I'll take you on.'

I whooped with delight and threw my hands up in the air. Unfortunately, I let go of the sword, and it flew across the garden, narrowly missing Stoutus but hitting and smashing a pot. Gaah.

'You can also tell him I'll be sending a separate bill for damages,' Stoutus said.

March XVII

I've spent the whole afternoon in the atrium practising my attacks. I can't believe I've got to wait two whole days for my next lesson.

When Dad came home, I showed him my moves and told him about how I was going to become a mighty hero.

After a couple of minutes, he went off to his room and sent a slave down to see me.

I asked the slave what was going on, and he said that Dad had put him on listening duty. I can't believe Dad off-loaded the task of listening to his own son to a slave. SO rude!

The slave sat there for a couple of hours. He smiled and nodded at first, but after a while his mouth started to sag and his hands trembled.

Eventually he ran out of the room shouting, 'I can't take it any more.'

What a silly, ungrateful little man. When you consider all the boring scrubbing and cleaning he usually has to do, you'd think it would be a treat to listen to me.

I told Dad to whip the slave, but he said he'd been punished enough for one night. I didn't really understand what he meant. Maybe he's already beaten him for something.

March XVIII

Cornelius, Gaius and Flavia came round this morning and I told them about my combat training. Cornelius must have been jealous because he kept teasing me about my out-of-date mosaic.

In the afternoon, we went to the forum for a game of hide and seek. I found a

really cool hiding place behind some baskets
of figs next to the sandal store, and
crouched into a tight ball.

When no one had found me after five
minutes, I was pretty pleased with myself.
But when they hadn't turned up after
twenty minutes ... not so great.

Sure enough, I walked back to the forum to see everyone pointing and laughing at me.

'We didn't even look for you,' sniggered Cornelius. 'We just wanted to see how long you'd wait before giving up. Happy Hilaria.'

Gaah! I had forgotten that Julius Caesar had announced that today was a special festival of Hilaria, when everyone gets to play pranks on each other. 'You can't play tricks on me,' I said. 'I'm going to be a mighty hero one day.'

'A mighty hero?' asked Cornelius. 'You'd be about as much use in a battle as a dead gladiator.'

I considered attacking him, but I thought I'd better wait until I'd had more training. So I walked away instead.

Gaius came running after me. 'Sorry about that,' he said. 'It was Cornelius's idea. He's been playing pranks all day. He tied my sandal straps together this morning, so you got off quite lightly, really.'

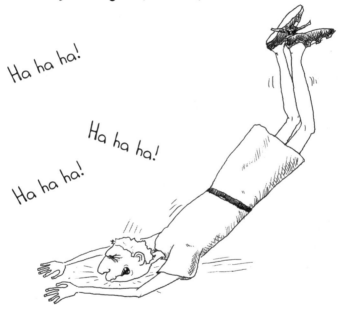

Ha ha ha!

Ha ha ha!

Ha ha ha!

I came up with a great Hilaria prank this evening. I went out into the garden, where I found a slave woman called Delia. I told her that we were short of money, so we were going to sell her to a slave trader.

I can't believe I kept a straight face. I'm MUCH better at jokes than Cornelius.

Maybe I'm a little too good, because Delia burst into tears and begged me to let her stay. I tried to explain it was just a trick, but this only made her wail louder.

Dad came rushing out to see what was happening. He made me apologize to Delia, which I thought was a bit much.

He NEVER apologizes to our slaves when he whips them. So why should I have to apologize for trying to liven things up with a practical joke?

March XIX

I had a great lesson about defending myself from attack today. Stoutus handed me a metal shield and explained how the army uses them to fight in a 'tortoise' formation.

Tortoise formation (correct)

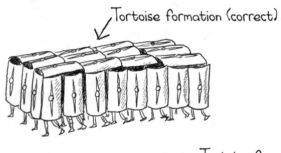

Tortoise formation (incorrect)

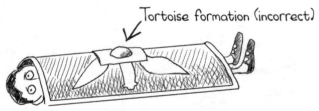

Tortoise

Unfortunately, the shield was so heavy it toppled over and pinned me to the ground. I pretty much looked like a tortoise, but I wouldn't have been much use in battle.

Stoutus got a big plate from his kitchen and told me to pretend it was a shield. Then he attacked me with a wooden sword and I had to dodge his blows.

It took me a while to get the hang of it, and Stoutus managed to land lots of hits on me. But he soon grew tired and slow.

He might have been a great fighter in his day, but now he runs out of energy pretty quickly and gets out of breath.

The lesson ended when I blocked an attack with so much force that the plate shattered. I was quite proud of my strength, despite the damage.

Stoutus said he'd add it to the bill. I must make sure I'm not around when Dad gets that.

HOW much?

March XX

DISASTER! I went to the barber today and now I have the most ridiculous haircut EVER.

'Give me the hairstyle of a noble Roman hero,' I demanded as I sat down.

The idiot then clipped the top of my head totally bald, and brushed the hair from the back of my head forward.

'What are you doing?' I asked.

'Giving you the hairstyle of a noble Roman hero,' he said. 'Julius Caesar, to be precise. He sweeps his hair forward to cover his baldness. He also wears a crown of laurel leaves to distract people. You should probably get one of those on your way home.'

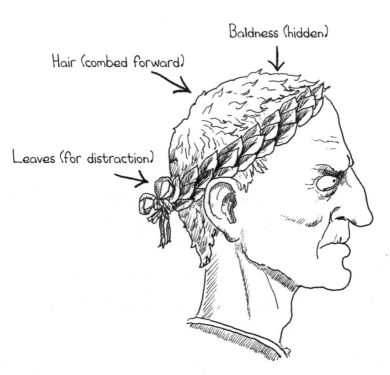

Baldness (hidden)

Hair (combed forward)

Leaves (for distraction)

'I can't walk around with leaves on my head,' I said. 'Everyone will tease me.'

'No one teases Caesar.'

'Of course no one teases Caesar. He's Caesar. He could wear a curly wig and a dress and no one would tease him.'

'Well, it's too late now, Dorkius,' said the barber. 'You'll have to be clearer next time.'

Like there's going to be a next time. I'd rather grow my hair long like a stinky barbarian than go back to that loser.

March XXI

Cornelius, Gaius and Flavia turned up today to see if I wanted to play hide and seek.

'No way,' I said. 'You'll only play tricks on me and tease me.'

'We won't,' said Gaius. 'That was just Cornelius, and he's stopped now.'

'It's true,' said Cornelius. 'I've not even mentioned your new hairstyle yet. That proves I've changed.'

'That's it,' I said. 'I'm NOT coming.'

'I'm only joking,' said Cornelius. 'I swear on my family's honour I won't do anything mean.'

When we got to the forum, Gaius counted first. I was about to run to the back of the bakery, when Cornelius dragged me a different way.

'I've found a brilliant new place to hide,' he whispered, leading me across a quiet street and down an alley between rows of tall townhouses. 'Let's hide down here,' he said, guiding me to a spot underneath a high window. 'Gaius'll never find us.'

So, like an idiot, I pressed myself against the wall, while Cornelius moved a little way away and giggled into his hand. I heard a rustling overhead and looked up to see a woman fling something out of a pot. Brown, gloopy stuff flew down. She was emptying poo out of a chamber pot. Gaah.

Repulsive poo

I darted aside like a swift gladiator, and the poo splattered down next to me. Thank the gods for my defence training. I'd never have managed to duck out of the way in time without it. Cornelius cracked up laughing.

'No, it missed me,' I shouted.

But then, right on cue, the woman threw out another potful. This time it splashed down the side of my leg. And Cornelius laughed even louder as I tried to shake off the brown sludge.

'I thought you swore on your family's honour that you wouldn't trick me,' I said.

'My family hasn't got any honour,' said Cornelius. 'They're even bigger losers than you.'

Then he ran over, lifted up my flap of hair, and slapped my forehead underneath it. I wonder if anyone does that to Julius Caesar? It would certainly explain all those wars he keeps starting.

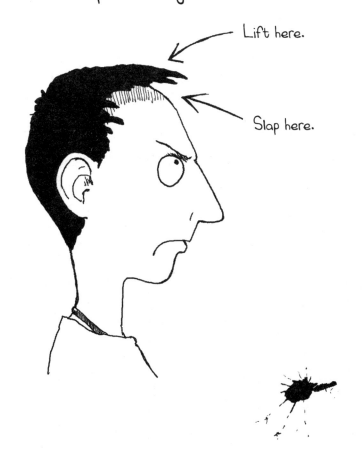

Lift here.

Slap here.

March XXII

More combat training today. As I was practising with the wooden sword, Stoutus told me all about the wars he has fought in.

Whenever Dad talks about his army days, he uses it as an excuse to drone on about glory and honour. But Stoutus tells me about cool, gory stuff like decimation, which is a punishment given to cowardly soldiers.

Ten soldiers

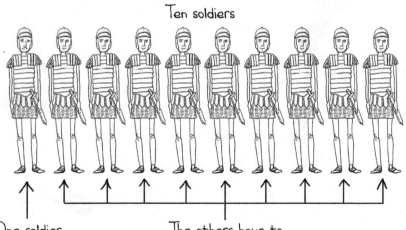

One soldier is chosen.

The others have to club him to death.

Pretty ruthless, eh? I hope I get to be ruthless one day.

Stoutus's army tales were really cool, so I asked if I could switch to a real sword. He made me promise to be extra careful, and then handed me a double-edged blade.

I held it up and tried to imagine all the barbarians he'd hacked with it. I called on the gods to make me as strong and fierce as Stoutus in his prime. Unfortunately, the gods either weren't listening or had better things to grant, because the sword slipped out of my hand and gashed my leg.

Stoutus said we should quit the training before I chopped my own head off and Dad murdered him in revenge. I said Dad would probably be more likely to thank him than kill him if that happened.

Thanks VERY much!

Stoutus asked if I wanted him to carry me home. My leg was hurting so much that I was tempted, but I didn't want to risk Cornelius seeing me, so I said I was fine and hopped back.

March XXIII

I smell like something that should be served up at a dinner party. Why? Because Mum noticed my leg this morning and raced off to fetch her doctor, Vibius.

He stumbled into my room and examined my leg. Then he fished a clump of unwashed lamb's wool out of his bag. It's his answer to everything — he probably gets it cheap somewhere.

Then Vibius went to work:

I. First he dipped the wool in vinegar, and rubbed it on my wound, which made it hurt a MILLION times worse.

II. Then he dabbed the wool in honey, and smeared it on my neck.

III. Then he dabbed it in egg yolk and wiped it down my arms.

IV. Finally, he tipped my head back and poured wine down my nostrils, which made me feel like I was drowning.

Afterwards, he looked at me and nodded, as if he'd just performed a miracle rather than coating me in random cooking ingredients. Mum thanked him and handed over a massive stack of coins.

And how does my leg feel after all that so-called treatment? Worse, of course.

March XXIV

Well, this is just great. Dad decided my combat lessons are too dangerous, so he cancelled them. Worse still, he brought boring Lucius back for another maths lesson.

I spent all morning staring at my pen and wishing it were a sword, so I could chop Lucius's head off. He must have sensed I was in a bad mood, because he kept giving me harder and harder sums to do.

Gaius came round this afternoon. I showed him my leg and told him I'd injured it in a sword fight. He seemed pretty impressed, but he'd have been less impressed if I'd mentioned that the fight was with MYSELF.

I told him about the prank Cornelius played, and he tutted. 'Cornelius has been acting like a complete pile of barbarian poo recently,' he said. 'Yesterday he wrote 'Gaius loves Flavia' on the wall opposite her house. Her dad went nuts.'

'Let's get revenge on him,' I said.

'We could make him wait under a window while someone empties their chamber pot,' suggested Gaius.

'No, we need to take things up to the next level,' I said. 'Let's tie raw meat to his arms and legs and throw him to a pack of wild dogs.'

Ruthless

What's wrong? I thought you liked hide and seek?

'Or we could write that HE loves Flavia on the wall opposite her house,' said Gaius.

It was obvious that Gaius isn't an original thinker like me, so I waited for him to go before I thought about the best way to get revenge.

March XXV

I've come up with a totally brilliant plan to get revenge on Cornelius. Here goes:

1. Gaius persuades Cornelius to play hide and seek in the large graveyard at the edge of town.

Cornelius   Gaius

II. On the way there,
Gaius tells Cornelius
that a ghost has
been spotted inside.

III. I cover my face
and arms with chalk
and wait behind the
gravestone opposite
the entrance.

IV. Gaius coughs
as they both
get near the
gravestone.

Ahem

V. I jump out and shout 'Woooo!'

VI. Cornelius's face turns even whiter than mine, and he pees his pants.

VII. I point and laugh. Everyone joins in.

March XXVI

I was supposed to be having more maths lessons today, but I had a headache so I told Mum I needed to rest. Unfortunately, this made her fetch Vibius again.

He examined my eyes, blasting me with his vile morning breath. 'This doesn't look good, Dorkius,' he said. 'Your eyes are watering, your skin is pale. You look very distressed.'

Vibius's disgusting morning breath

Watering eyes

Pale skin

Fear

Of course my eyes are watering, my skin is pale and I look distressed, I thought. I just got a whiff of your stinky dog breath. Do you use the wiping stick as a toothbrush?

Vibius tapped the side of my head. 'No doubt about it. There's a ghost trapped in there.'

'Thank the gods you came in time,' said Mum.

'This is very simple. I just need to make a small hole in the side of your head so the ghost can escape,' said Vibius, taking a small saw out of his bag.

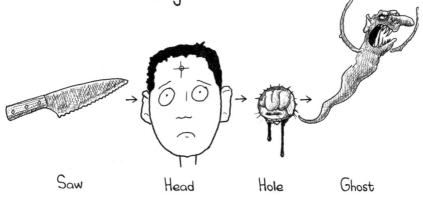

Saw   Head   Hole   Ghost

A ghost in my head? What was the old fool talking about? He staggered forward and dropped his saw. I wouldn't let him operate on me even if I did want a hole in my head.

I leapt off the couch, saying, 'You know what? I'm feeling better now, and I won't need any treatment. Time for my maths lesson, isn't it?'

'That's a shame,' said Vibius. 'I can still do the hole if you want. I'll even do it for half price.'

'No thanks,' I said, shoving him towards the door.

My maths lesson was even more unbearable than usual. But at least I don't have a hole in my skull. You know it's been a rubbish day when that's the best you can say.

March XXVII

My headache has gone now. I bet Vibius would say that the ghost has crawled out through one of my nostrils.

Or maybe Vibius doesn't know what the Tartarus he's talking about. I wonder if someone has sawn a hole in the side of HIS head and made his brains leak out.

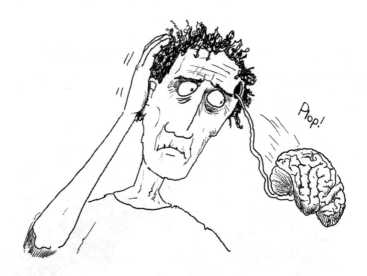

Plop!

Gaius came round again today, and I told him all about my plan to get revenge on Cornelius. He said it was totally brilliant. We're all set to do it tomorrow.

It sounds like Cornelius is getting worse and worse. Apparently, he invented a game called 'poo chase' yesterday. He stole a wiping stick from the public toilets and tried to poke everyone with it.

March XXVIII

I got to the graveyard just before noon
and crouched behind the tomb opposite the
entrance. A minute later, I heard a couple
of men strolling towards me. They stopped
right in front of the tomb.

Brilliant. How was I supposed to jump out
with these idiots blocking my way?

'It's nearly time,' said a man with a very
high voice. 'We need to be ready to strike
Baldy as soon as we get the word.'

'I'm ready,' said a man with a very low voice.
'He won't be making a nuisance of himself
once I've finished with him.'

The men walked on, but I was busy
wondering what they meant. Who was

Baldy? Why was he a nuisance? I was so distracted by this that I must have missed Gaius's first few coughs. By the time I snapped out of it, Gaius sounded like he was choking on a fish bone.

I leapt out and shouted, 'WOOOOO.' Unfortunately, it wasn't Cornelius I was yelling at, but the seriously terrified face of an old lady.

'Honorius?' she asked. 'Is that you? Why have you come back from the dead? Didn't we bury you properly?'

'Er, I'm not Honorius,' I said. 'Sorry. I was just hiding there as a joke.'

The woman grabbed me by the ear. 'Is that your idea of a joke? Pretending to be my dead son and hiding behind his grave?'

'I'm sorry. I didn't mean it.'

The woman yanked on my ear ... really hard.

'Stop!' I shouted. 'That REALLY hurts.'

Just then I noticed Cornelius. He was standing nearby with Gaius and Flavia, and they were all killing themselves laughing.

March XXIX

My leg's healed now, although my ear still
hurts from all the pulling. I need to get
back to my training.

But Dad was really odd when I asked him.
He didn't agree to start my lessons again,
but he WAS interested in what I was
saying for once. Very interested, in fact.

He was reading in the atrium and ignored me as usual when I started telling him about my failed prank. But when I got to the bit about the two men I'd overheard, Dad threw his scroll on the floor and grabbed me by the shoulders.

He made me repeat what the men said over and over and OVER again. Then he told me what he thought the two men were discussing ...

It's TOP TOP TOP SECRET.

It's so top secret that I had to promise never to mention it to ANYONE, and not even write it here. So I'm going to have to stop writing right now ...

March XXX

Arggh! Not telling my secret is so annoying. I'm going to have to write about it here and hide this scroll behind my bed every night. Otherwise I'll BURST.

Here goes ... Dad thinks I overheard a plot to murder Julius Caesar. 'Baldy' is the nickname some senators use for him because of the dumb hairstyle he shares with me.

According to Dad, Caesar has loads of enemies because he keeps making important decisions without asking anyone else. Some of Caesar's enemies must have hired assassins to bump him off. But which ones?

I asked Dad what would happen if Caesar was murdered. He said that Rome would collapse into chaos, blood would run in the streets and we'd have to flee to the countryside where they don't have any stuff like gladiator fights or chariot races. Boring!

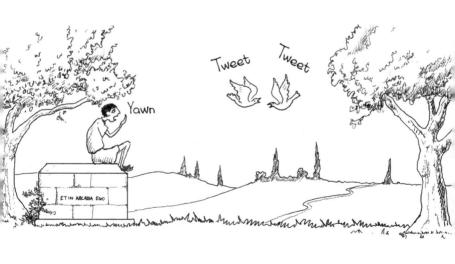

95

So now Dad has me wandering around Rome until I find the men with the high and low voices again.

Will I find them? I doubt it. There are three-quarters of a million people in Rome. I can't listen to ALL of them. But Dad won't let me restart my training unless I try.

March XXXI

Well that was a MASSIVE waste of time.
I wandered around for hours, dodging falling
poo in alleyways all over Rome. I listened
and listened, got some seriously odd looks
from people who thought I was just being
nosy, but didn't hear the voices again.

When I failed, Dad went on and on about
how much danger we'd be in if Caesar was
killed. I said this was all the more reason
to restart my training, which I thought
was quite a clever way of bringing the
conversation back round to what I wanted.

He told me to ask Mum if I could train
again, and she told me to ask her chickens.
Typical. This is the MOST important
decision Mum and Dad need to make about
my life right now, and they want to leave it

to a couple of useless flightless birds. Are chickens going to decide EVERYTHING now?

April I

The Good News: The chickens ate their grain last night, so I was allowed to start my training again.

The Bad News: Mum heard an owl screeching, which she took as a bad omen, so now training is on hold again.

Hey, would any other birds like to comment on my life? Perhaps there's a pigeon out there that doesn't like my dress sense? Or maybe there's a crow that wants to complain about my choice of friends?

That loudmouth owl had better stop hooting omens. If it tries it again, IT will be the one heading for bad luck.

Why won't Dad ever buy me what I want?
He's happy to let Mum buy countless sacred
chickens and pigs. But whenever I want
something, he pretends he didn't hear me, or
claims we've got no money.

We went down to the auction to buy a new
slave today, and Dad insisted on buying the
cheapest one.

There was a Greek kid called Linos who
was my age and could speak Latin. I asked
Dad if we could buy him so I could talk
to him about my combat training, but he
refused. He said it would be a waste of
money as we already had plenty of slaves
who could speak Latin. But we don't have
any MY age, do we?

We ended up buying a woman who was
about a HUNDRED years old. Dad thought

he was getting a bargain, but he needs to think long-term. As soon as that woman works hard, she's going to keel over and need replacing. Linos might have been twice the money, but he'd last FIVE times longer.

Which would YOU buy?

Latin speaking

Only speaks Greek.

My age

Old

Strong

Weak

As we wandered home with our ungrateful new slave muttering to herself in Greek, I asked Dad what would happen to Linos.

'He might end up working from dawn until dusk in a stone quarry, but he'd probably STILL prefer it to hearing your boring stories, Dorkius,' said Dad.

Ha ha, I DON'T think.

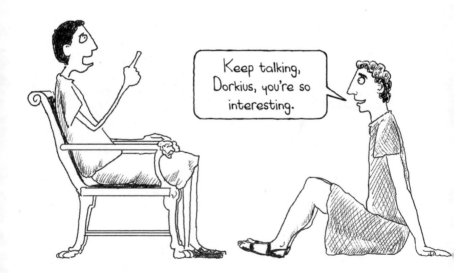

April 11

I went down to the public bathhouse this afternoon. I was just relaxing on a bench, enjoying the soothing steam, when I heard a couple of men chatting on the other side of the room.

At first I didn't pay them much attention. But after a while their voices started to sound familiar.

'Not long now,' said a man with a very high voice. 'Make sure you're ready.'

'It had better be soon,' said a man with a very deep voice. 'I've turned down some good torture work from the money-lenders for this.'

It was them. The men I'd heard in the graveyard were RIGHT HERE.

The room was too steamy for me to see anything, so I dashed over to where the voices had come from. Then I yelped in pain and rushed back. The floor was SERIOUSLY hot.

I put my sandals on and crossed the floor again. There was no one there.

The men had gone, but they couldn't have got far. I was going to find them and save Rome from disaster.

I searched all around the baths. I checked all the pools, gardens and massage rooms, but I couldn't see them.

Just as I was about to give up, I heard the voices again. Two men were making their way out of the exit. This is what they looked like, just in case I forget them:

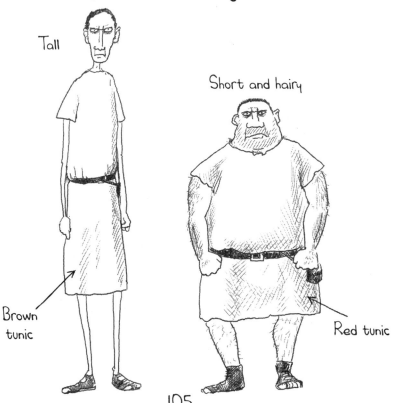

Tall

Short and hairy

Brown tunic

Red tunic

I ran after the men, and got outside just in time to see them turning into an alleyway. I wanted to keep going, but something felt wrong ... it seemed very cold for midday.

Oops. I'd left all my clothes in the changing room. The SHAME! I tried to cover myself up and sidestepped back to the baths. Even worse, Cornelius, Gaius and Flavia chose that exact moment to walk past.

Heat from baths

Heat from embarrassment

Why do the gods hate me?

April III

When I told Dad what happened yesterday,
he said I should have chased after the men
even though I had no clothes on. No way.
I want to save Julius Caesar, but not if it
means running around the streets of Rome
stark naked.

Dad thinks it'll be easier to find the men
now I know what they look like, and he sent
me out to look for them again.

It didn't really make things any easier, of
course. I knew one of them was short and
the other was tall, but it didn't narrow
things down much. I spent all day looking for
the men.

I DID see someone I recognized, though
— Linos, the Greek kid. He works for the

laundry now, and was carrying a huge pot of wee. It was really full, TOTALLY gross, and wee kept splashing over the sides on to his ragged clothes.

Fresh wee

Stale wee

'Sorry we couldn't buy you,' I said. 'Dad never forks out for good stuff. I've been bugging him for a bronze model of a chariot for years, and he still hasn't bought it.'

'Never mind,' said Linos. 'Things could be worse.'

'You're carrying a massive pot of wee around,' I said. 'How could things possibly be worse?'

'I'm learning a trade,' said Linos. 'I can already tell which wee will work best just from the smell. Besides, the other boy they bought has to stamp on the clothes in the washtub. Compared to that, this is luxury.'

April IV

I went to the amphitheatre this afternoon. Julius Caesar had some prisoners paraded in front of him. He scowled at them, then raised his hand. Executioners pulled ropes tight around their necks, and the prisoners choked and gurgled until they fell limply.

I thought it was all pretty gross, but the crowd rose to their feet and cheered.

Dad says Caesar always kills a few war prisoners if he's worried he's losing the people's support, as he knows how much they love a good execution.

After that, it was time for the fights.

The Bad News: My new favourite gladiator, Flamma, was killed by one called Rutuba.

The Good News: Rutuba has a trident and a net just like Triumphus, so the mosaic on my floor is totally up-to-date again. I just need to change the name on it.

April V

Dad told me to lash one of the slaves tonight. He reckons Odius, one of our older slaves, has grown lazy and needs to be taught a lesson. Dad usually does it himself, but he was busy working on a speech for the senate.

I pretended I was too tired, but he told me to stop being a coward and face my responsibility.

'Your brother loved beating slaves when he was your age. Sometimes he'd punish them just for looking at him in a funny way.'

Gaah! Brawnus does everything better than me. Dad reckons Brawnus's first word was 'battle', whereas mine was 'flower', but I'm sure he made that one up.

Baby Brawnus

Baby Dorkius

It was time to prove Dad wrong. I grabbed the lash and called Odius into the garden.

Odius slouched over from the slaves' quarters, chewing on a stale crust of bread and scratching his stomach.

'I've been told you haven't been pulling your rather large weight,' I said. 'So I need to beat you.'

Odius sniggered. 'Good joke, Dorkius. You almost had me there.'

I cracked the lash to show him I meant business. Odius's eyes widened and he dropped the bread.

'Please don't whip me. I promise I'll try harder,' he snivelled.

'The time for excuses has passed,' I said. 'The time for ruthlessness has arrived.'

I'd love to tell you I whipped Odius, but I just couldn't. I looked at his shaking hands and wobbling lip. He'd obviously got the message.

'Alright,' I said. 'Just scream as loudly as you can, so it sounds like I'm whipping you.'

Odius screamed so loudly I had to cover my ears. It was the hardest I'd ever seen him work.

Not THAT loud, I'm not supposed to be killing you.

Aaaaaarrrrgggh!

Afterwards, I returned the whip, and Dad said I'd done my duty well. At least HE was convinced by Odius's performance.

Now I'm worried I'm not ruthless enough to be a true Roman hero. Maybe I should start with something smaller, like stamping on a mouse. But what if it has baby mice who will be sad if it dies?

It's not easy being ruthless.

April VI

Terrific news ... Dad is letting me restart training. He was so proud of me for whipping Odius he gave in. Stoutus has agreed to take me back, although he's demanded extra money to make up for all the stress.

What stress? His body is covered with scars from fierce battles. What harm could I do to him?

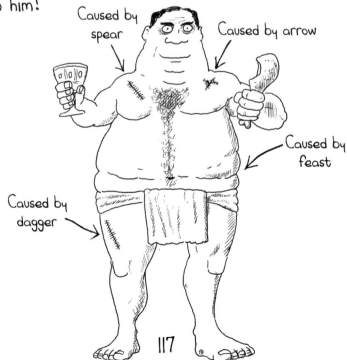

Caused by spear

Caused by arrow

Caused by feast

Caused by dagger

Maybe he senses I'm going to be a mighty hero, and he's frightened of unleashing my power.

April VII

Dad made me get up earlier than the slaves so I could go on another pointless search for the assassins.

But training made up for it. Stoutus let me fight him today. He insisted on wearing armour. What did he expect me to do with my wooden sword? Give him a fatal splinter?

Not that the armour gave him much protection anyway. His massive stomach pushed the two halves apart, straining the ties and hooks to breaking point.

Stoutus was very quick at first. With his first strike, he pressed his wooden sword into my chest and said, 'Dead.'

Massive stomach

I spun round, but he jabbed the sword into the small of my back and said, 'Really dead.'

I tried sneaking up behind him, but he pushed the sword against my neck and said, 'Really, really dead.'

After a while, Stoutus's tunic got all wet with sweat patches and he slowed down. He paused to catch his breath, and I struck

my sword into his stomach. NOT a small target, but I still felt proud of landing a blow on such a military legend.

Unfortunately, the force of the strike made Stoutus burp. GROSS!

Toxic

Burp!

It was like an inbuilt defence to blast attackers with rotten chicken-breath. I staggered backwards, my eyes streaming from the stench. Stoutus swung his sword into my chest and said, 'This time you're really, really, REALLY dead.'

April VIII

I killed Stoutus today.

Okay, I didn't actually kill him, but I pressed my wooden sword right into his chest, which would have totally finished him off in a real battle.

Stoutus was very quick at first, but he soon grew slow and sweaty again. I whacked my sword into his with such force that it went spinning across the floor.

I shoved my sword through the gap in his armour. 'This time YOU'RE the one who's dead,' I said.

'It doesn't count. My armour isn't on properly,' said Stoutus.

'Of course it isn't on properly,' I said. 'You'd have to cut out feasting for a month if you wanted to do it up.'

'Nonsense,' said Stoutus. 'Anyway, it's good to have a layer of fat to protect yourself in battle. Harder for swords to get through.'

Yeah, and you can always sit on your enemies, I wanted to say. But I decided I might really end up dead if I said it out loud.

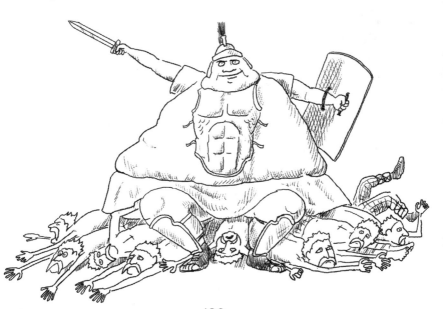

April IX

Dad decided HE'D go and look for the assassins today, because I wasn't doing it right. Not sure how he is going to recognize voices he has NEVER heard.

I, on the other hand, had my first ever riding lesson. As Stoutus led me into his stables to pick a horse, they all reared up and whinnied. I thought this might be a bad omen, but then I realized they were just worried Stoutus was going to sit on them and crush them.

One of the horses had a mane that swept forward over its head just like Caesar's hair. I took this as a sign that he was a horse fit for a mighty hero.

Same

'That's Candidus,' said Stoutus. 'Good choice. Hop on.'

I'd never been on a horse before, and I had no idea how to mount one. My face was level with its back. Was I supposed to leap as high as my head and land on top?

I hung on to Candidus's back and tried to swing my legs up, but I just kicked him and made him bolt across the field.

Stoutus ran after the horse and brought him back. He tried holding on to one of my feet while I lifted the other over Candidus's back. I flapped around, while Stoutus pushed up with all his strength. Finally, I stretched my leg over and clambered on.

At last, I was a noble rider in the cavalry. I was ready to charge into battle. Oh, I was facing the wrong way.

Stoutus pulled me down and said we'd try again tomorrow.

April X

Stoutus ordered three slaves to join us in the field today. One of them was very short, one very tall, and the other was normal height.

They crouched down next to Candidus, creating a set of weird human stairs for me to climb. Pretty embarrassing, but I was so excited about riding a horse I didn't care.

I kicked my legs into Candidus's sides, and we were off. Stoutus told me how to steer with the reins as we trotted around the field.

I rode round and round all day, as Stoutus chewed on a plate of goose livers. At the end of the lesson, he said I was a natural rider and I beamed with pride.

Every day I get closer to becoming a proper Roman hero. Now all I need to do is catch the assassins, save Rome, and grow as tall as my brother.

The slaves had to form the human steps again so I could get off. I apologized to the tallest one, but he said he didn't mind.

He said Stoutus had stood on him to mount Candidus once, and he was so heavy it was like being trampled by a horse. Compared to Stoutus, I was pretty easy work.

Groan!

April XI

I had a day off from searching today and we went to a chariot race. Because of Dad's job, we got to sit on marble seats at the front. Some people get up at dawn to queue for good seats, but we just strolled right in and got a great view.

The moment we sat down, the gates swung open and the chariots thundered out.

My riding lessons have given me a new respect for charioteers. If I find it hard just to get on a horse, steering four of them around those crazy bends in the circuit must be pretty tough.

We support the white team, but they never seem to win. I've asked Dad if I can switch teams, but he said proper chariot fans are loyal fans. There were twelve races today, and our team lost ALL of them.

We almost won the last race, but the blue team overtook right at the end.

Some of our fans accused the blue fans of putting a curse on our racer, and a fight broke out in the stands.

As a reward for winning the race, a horse from the blue team was sacrificed to the god Mars – a pretty strange reward. If I was one of those horses I'd WANT to lose.

April XII

Stamina training today.

April XIII

I was way too tired to write anything last night. Stoutus said that soldiers in the legions have to march over twenty miles a day with heavy packs on. He decided he was going to teach me to do the same.

He wanted me to march with a full backpack, but I couldn't even stand up with it on, so he let me practise with an empty one instead.

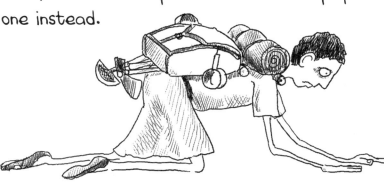

I walked round and round the field until the ache in my legs, arms and shoulders got unbearable. At lunchtime, Stoutus brought out a plate of honey dormice. I thought he'd let me stop for lunch, but he told me to keep going.

Every time I passed the plate of delicious dormice, my stomach rumbled.

When Stoutus had finished, he tossed the plate on the ground and started picking his nose and eating it for dessert. After a while even the sight of his bogeys made my stomach rumble. THAT's how hungry I was.

As the afternoon wore on, I got so tired, I started seeing black spots in front of my eyes. Every time I passed Stoutus, I asked if I could stop. He said things like:

I kept on marching until the sun started to go down.

One of Stoutus's servants brought him three huge plates of chicken for his dinner, but he didn't offer me a SINGLE piece.

He even looked like he was struggling to eat them all, and he was as sweaty as me by the time he'd finished them.

Soon after the sun had set, my legs wobbled, and I collapsed into a heap. Stoutus came over and prodded me with his sandal.

'That'll do for today,' he said. 'A decent effort, Dorkius.'

Dad was having another noisy dinner party when I finally hobbled back home. Usually all the belching, vomiting and shouting keeps me awake, but this time I went straight to sleep.

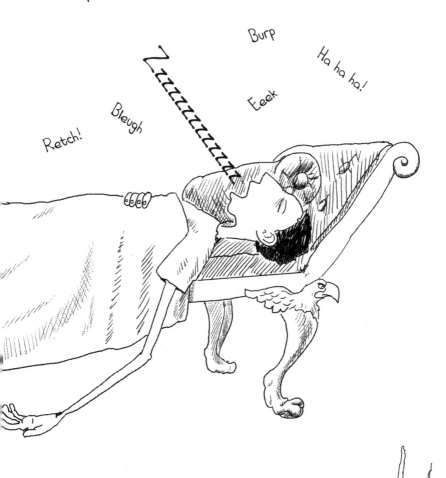

April XIV

That was strange. When I went round to see Stoutus today, he said he had to put my training on hold and sent me home.

I wandered off, trying to work out why he didn't want to teach me any more. But then I remembered what he'd said in my stamina lesson: 'A real hero never gives up, no matter what anyone says.'

Ah, it was all part of my training — Stoutus was just testing me to see if I had a hero's attitude. I'll go back tomorrow and DEMAND more lessons.

Wow, you're becoming a real hero, Dorkius.

April XV

When I got to Stoutus's house this morning, his servant said he wasn't in. I knew he was lying, because I could hear Stoutus's voice coming from the garden, so I sneaked round to the back gate.

I could hear two men talking to Stoutus. One of them had a very high voice, and one of them had a very low voice.

THE ASSASSINS! I dashed along to the back gate and peeked through the slats.

It was definitely them. But how could I
warn Stoutus that he was mixing with
seriously evil criminals?

It turns out I didn't need to.

'Baldy has just set out for his villa with only
two bodyguards,' said the man with the high
voice. 'There'll be no one else around if we
strike now. This is our chance.'

'We'll take the guards out, and you go
after Baldy,' said the deep-voiced man.

'Okay,' said Stoutus. 'But he'll be a tough swine to kill. I'll need your help when you've killed the bodyguards.'

I heard them running to the stables and mounting their horses. Hooves thundered across the garden and the gate flew open. I squashed myself against the wall and watched them gallop off.

At first I tried to convince myself it was all still some kind of test, but I had to face facts. Stoutus was part of a conspiracy to murder Julius Caesar, and I was the ONLY person who knew.

First I thought I'd run to the senate and tell Dad. But even if I got past the guards and persuaded him to come, we'd be too late to save Caesar.

No. If I wanted to stop the murder, I'd have to do it myself. It would mean taking on an ex-soldier and two professional assassins. I had about as much chance of succeeding as a dormouse trying to stop a chariot.

Stop!

But I had to try. At least I'd definitely get into Elysium if I died trying to save Caesar. I'd be the noblest hero of all time.

NOBLE HEROES

I ran to the stables. Candidus was still there, thank the gods. I let him out of his stall, but how was I going to mount him by myself? I could hardly ask the servants to help me steal their master's horse.

Just then, Candidus wandered over to a tree at the edge of the garden and stood underneath it. GENIUS.

I climbed up the trunk, pulled myself along an overhanging branch and dropped down on to Candidus's back.

A couple of servants came out to see what was going on, so I squeezed my legs into the horse's side, and we sped out through the gate.

I held my fist high in the air and let out a mighty battle roar as we charged off. Then I realized I had absolutely no idea where I was going and stopped roaring.

RRRRROOOOAAARRRRR ... oh.

As we thundered over a hill, I spotted a wagon making its way along a path at the bottom. As I got closer, I recognized the boy sitting on the back. It was Linos, the Greek kid, and he was squashed between a couple of overflowing wee pots.

I waved at the driver, who pulled the wagon to a stop. Linos looked up.

'It's me, Dorkius,' I said. 'The one whose dad was too mean to buy you. Listen, I need to get to Caesar's villa. Do you know where it is?'

'Who?' asked Linos.

'How can you not know who Julius Caesar is? He's only the most famous person in the world. He's got a hairstyle like this horse and he wears leaves on his head.'

Linos thought for a moment. 'Oh yeah,' he said. 'I know him. I've collected his wee a few times. Very strong stuff. He must have a very rich diet.'

'Where's his villa?' I asked.

Linos pointed over my shoulder. 'He lives on that hill.'

'Excellent,' I said. 'Now you must listen to me very carefully. Some men are about to kill Julius Caesar, and I've got to stop them. I'm probably going to fail, but at least I'll die a hero's death. So please can you go to the senate and tell my dad I found the men I was looking for, and I died a hero's death? Do you understand?'

Linos looked confused, but finally he nodded, and I raced away in the direction he'd pointed.

As I approached the hill, I saw a stream flowing at the foot of it.

'Jump the stream, Candidus,' I shouted, sure he would understand.

Candidus came to a firm halt at the edge of the stream, and I went flying into it.

As I splashed around, Candidus wandered off to munch some grass. I'd have to leave the stupid beast behind and continue on foot.

I ran up the hill so fast I got a stitch in my side, and wanted to sit down. But then I remembered what Stoutus had said: 'A true Roman hero never quits.'

Mind you, if he'd known I'd use this advice to attack him, he'd probably have said: 'A true Roman hero realizes it isn't worth the hassle, and goes home for a nice rest.'

Eventually I saw the villa up ahead. A guard was lying face down in a pool of blood in front of the main gate.

I was too late to save him. But was I too late to help Caesar?

I heard cries and the sounds of a struggle coming from inside.

I flipped over the guard's body. He'd been stabbed before he'd even drawn his sword. If they'd killed a trained bodyguard so easily, what chance did I have?

It didn't matter. I HAD to try. I pulled the guard's sword out of its scabbard and held it up as I entered.

There was a blur of movement on the far side of the atrium. The tall man and the short man were circling Caesar's last-remaining bodyguard.

The guard turned from left to right to left again, flinging his sword around, but he missed both the men.

The tall man nipped forward and plunged his sword into the guard's back. The guard yelped and dropped his sword.

The short man thrust his sword deep into the guard's chest and he sank down to the floor, flapped about like a fish on a chopping table, and then he was really still.

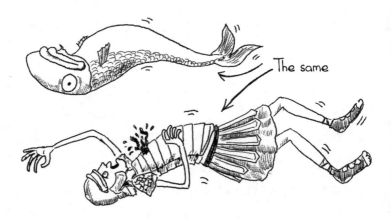

The same

Julius Caesar was pressed against the wall on the other side of the atrium, holding out his sword as Stoutus crept towards him.

Caesar's laurel wreath had fallen off and his hair had flopped open, leaving the top of his head exposed. Maybe he was hoping to blind Stoutus with the glare from his shiny bald patch.

Gleaming blade

Gleaming head

Just then Stoutus spotted me.

'Get out of here,' he shouted. 'This is serious business. I don't want your help.'

'I'm not here to help,' I shouted. 'I'm here to stop you. I am a noble Roman hero and I demand that you surrender.'

I meant this to sound forceful, but my voice came out all squeaky. My palms were so sweaty I dropped the sword, and had to scrabble around to pick it up.

Stoutus shook his head and laughed, which gave Caesar a split second. He lunged forward and stabbed Stoutus in the gut. Stoutus thudded to the ground like a wounded elephant.

The assassins rushed for Caesar. He defended himself against both of them at

once, ducking from side to side and jabbing
his sword out with incredible speed. Pretty
impressive moves for an old guy.

'Step away from our noble leader,' I shouted,
running across the floor.

Stoutus lurched up and blocked my path.
He was clutching his wound with one hand,
and he looked even paler and sweatier
than that time he'd scoffed three plates
of chicken.

He swung his sword at me, but I ducked out
of the way.

'Thanks for the defence lessons,' I said. 'And
the combat ones.'

This would have been quite a clever
remark if I'd managed to stab him straight
afterwards. Unfortunately, he blocked my
attack easily.

'You think you can beat your teacher after
just a few lessons?' laughed Stoutus. 'How

many times did I kill you? Fifty? A hundred?
And now I only have to kill you once.'

Stoutus was right. He had years of battle
experience and I had a few hours of
training. But if I kept moving, I could tire
him out. And then I'd have a chance.

Stoutus lunged again, and I leapt back. Unfortunately, I slipped on a puddle of blood and fell flat on my back. Stoutus stepped up and prodded his sword into my chest.

'This time you're really, really, really, REALLY dead,' he said.

I stared at the sword, waiting for it to thrust into my heart. This is it, I thought. A moment of agony and then I'll see the black waters of the River Styx.

I wasn't frightened of the pain. I really wasn't. But I was seriously worried I wouldn't get into Elysium because I'd failed to save Caesar.

I closed my eyes and gritted my teeth.

Nothing happened.

I opened my eyes and looked up at Stoutus. I thought he was about to speak, but all that came from his lips was a trickle of blood.

Then the tip of a sword poked through his stomach and he collapsed on top of me.
A final cloud of toxic chicken-breath blasted out of Stoutus's mouth and he fell still.

I knew all that stuff about fat protecting you from attack was nonsense.

Toxic breath blast

I could hear sandals slapping across flagstones, but I couldn't see anything. Stoutus's body was pinning me to the floor, and I couldn't move.

Swords clanked and a man screamed in agony, but I had no idea who it was. I cried out for help, but just then I heard a very familiar voice.

'Alright, Dorkius. I'll get to you in a minute.'

It was Dad.

Another scream, and then silence.

I saw Dad's feet approaching. He lifted Stoutus's body off me, and I looked around.

The tall man and the short man were both lying on the floor with swords sticking out of their chests. It looked like they'd be returning to the graveyard really soon, but not for any secret conversations.

Caesar and Dad had dark red splashes on their togas, but they were okay.

'You saved my life, boy,' said Caesar, then he turned to my dad. 'Your son is a true Roman hero, Gluteus Maximus.'

WOW! I hope those afterlife judges were listening. Did you get that, guys? Caesar reckons I'm a hero. I must be absolutely guaranteed a place in Elysium now.

One free pass to Elysium for the hero Dorkius Maximus.

Caesar picked his crown of leaves from the floor and swept his hair over the front of his head. 'Don't tell anyone about my hair problems,' he said.

Er, right. Like anyone's convinced by that silly flap of hair he brushes forward.

I wandered over to Stoutus and took out a coin.

'Here's something to pay the ferryman with so he'll take you over the River Styx,' I said, placing it under his tongue. 'I know you tried to kill me, but you were a good teacher, and I still hope you get into Elysium. Try not to sink the ferry on the way.'

April XVII

Didn't write yesterday as I spent all day repeating my story over and over again to men from the senate.

Caesar was surprisingly calm, but everyone else was really stressed. The senators kept asking if the assassins had mentioned anyone else who was involved in the plot.

Er, no one mentioned MY name, did they?

I couldn't work out if they really wanted to get to the bottom of it or were just worried their own names had been mentioned.

Eventually, they let me go. I didn't catch up with Dad until this afternoon. He told me how he'd been sitting in the senate when a boy carrying an overflowing pot of wee rushed in.

Intruders wouldn't normally get in, but the guards were so disgusted by the smell they failed to grab him.

Linos gave Dad a crazy message about strange men at Caesar's villa, and he decided to investigate.

Dad asked some of the other senators to come along, but they didn't seem interested, so he leapt on his horse and rode to the villa alone. He got there just in time to save me from Stoutus and help Caesar.

Dad said I showed great courage in chasing the assassins. I expected him to add something like 'Your brother would have killed them all without my help', but it never came.

All Mum seemed to care about was the bloodstains on Dad's toga, though. 'Look at these,' she said. 'I'll need some really expensive wee to get them out.'

'Don't you care that we saved Rome?' I asked.

'Of course I do, Dorky Worky,' she said. 'You did very well. But the chickens would have warned us if there was any real danger.'

I saw no point in arguing. Mum obviously cares more about her chickens than me. Maybe she'd like to ask them to protect our glorious leader next time he's in trouble.

April XVIII

Dad took me down to the forum this afternoon. He said I could choose a present for saving Caesar, but I couldn't find anything I liked.

I looked at that bronze chariot statue I used to want, but I didn't really like it any more. Even chariot racing doesn't seem that exciting when you've done some proper heroic stuff.

I wandered past a slave auction at the edge of the forum and stopped. I couldn't believe it. Linos was up for sale AGAIN.

'What happened?' I asked.

'My master's getting rid of me because I abandoned my duty,' said Linos.

'Didn't you explain to him how important it was? Didn't you tell him that Rome would have collapsed into chaos and violence?'

'I tried,' said Linos. 'But he said that chaos would be a good thing. The bloodshed would stain everyone's togas, which would be seriously good for business.'

I dashed back to Dad, and told him I'd found the thing I really wanted. He was quite annoyed that it was a slave, but he kept his promise and forked out for Linos.

It was just as well, because a man from one of the stone quarries was examining Linos. He'd have snapped him up if we weren't there.

Linos came back home with us, and I spent all evening explaining to him how he'd helped me save Rome. Unlike our other ungrateful slaves, Linos actually enjoys listening to me, and asked to hear the story over and over again.

If only Dad hadn't been so stingy in the first place, I'd have had someone to talk to all along.

April XIX

Amazing news. Caesar is letting me ride in the parade tomorrow.

He's going to ride through the crowds in a golden chariot, and, as a reward for saving his life, he's asked me and Dad to follow in our own chariot.

Tomorrow is going to be the coolest day EVER.

Dad came into my room tonight and asked what I was going to wear. Eh? Doesn't he know I always wear my tunic, except for when it's being washed in wee?

But then he pulled out a toga. My first EVER toga. I'd thought I'd have to wait a

couple of years to get one of those, but
Dad says I've proved I'm ready.

Wow ... togas are really heavy, and seriously
hard to put on.

Wrong

Wrong

Wrong

RIGHT!

Even when I'd finally got it on, it made my left arm ache really badly. But it's fine — I'm a hero now. I survived that awful stitch in my side when I was running to save Caesar, so I'm sure I can put up with a slight pain in my arm.

April XX

Even if I'd only seen it from the crowd, today's parade would have been amazing, but watching it from a chariot was totally BRILLIANT.

The crowd was HUGE. I couldn't believe how many people were crammed on to the streets, waving, cheering and throwing flowers.

A group of senators with three white oxen led the procession.

I get the feeling this isn't going to end well.

Caesar was next in a golden chariot drawn by white horses. A slave stood behind Caesar. Dad said his job was to remind

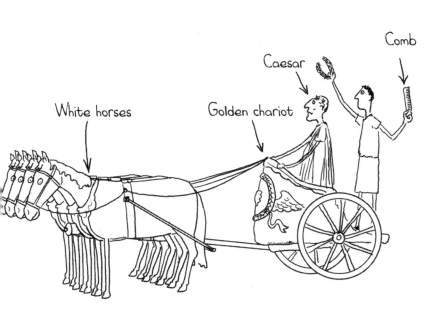

White horses

Golden chariot

Caesar

Comb

Caesar that he was just a human and not a god. I reckon his real job was to make sure Caesar's hair didn't flap around in the wind and give the crowd a good laugh.

Further back, there were loads of animals — elephants and some crazy creatures with long necks called 'giraffes'. Cornelius told me about them once, but I thought it was just another trick, like the giant killer mouse and the three-headed sheep he told me about.

Giraffe
– real

Giant killer
mouse – not real

Three-headed sheep
– not real

I even spotted Cornelius and Gaius on a
street corner. I waved at them, and both
their mouths dropped open in shock. Cornelius
rushed forward to check it was really me,
but he slipped and fell into a pile of fresh
donkey poo.

Ha ha

Ha ha

Embarrassment

Eventually, we made our way up Capitol Hill to the Temple of Jupiter, where a priest sacrificed the oxen. I wanted to rush home and tell Linos all about it, but Dad said there was someone he wanted to show me.

He led me to some soldiers at the bottom of the temple steps. One of them turned round and smiled. I couldn't believe it ... it was Brawnus.

Squeeeeeze

He hugged me and said he'd heard I was a true Roman hero now. I think that was my proudest moment EVER.

April XXI

Brawnus is staying with us for a few days while his legion is on leave. I spent all day in the garden listening to his war stories.

We're having a banquet tonight to celebrate Brawnus's return, and I'm going to stuff my face with cows' udders, squid stuffed with calves' brains, goose livers and honey dormice.

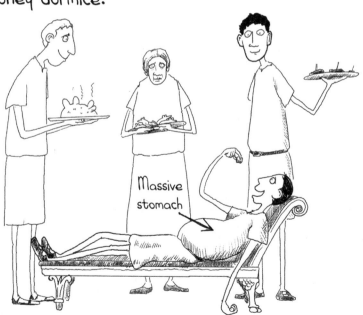

Massive stomach

April XXII

The feast was amazing last night, and I stayed up right until the end.

I'd just piled my plate with lovely food, when Dad tickled the back of his throat with a feather and threw up into his pot. Some of the vomit splashed on to my plate, so I had to throw it all away and start again.

Lovely food   Unwanted topping

After that, I stood in the corner to eat, where I was safe from all the rebounding spew.

This morning I sat in the garden with Brawnus and Dad, having a marvellous time talking about heroic things, until Mum came rushing out with tears streaming down her cheeks.

'My priest has foreseen a great tragedy. It will take place on the Ides of March next year.'

Only the gods know why she gets herself into such a state. The Ides of March is ages away, so I'm sure this 'tragedy' will all have worked itself out by then.

You mark my words. The Ides of March will be fine ...

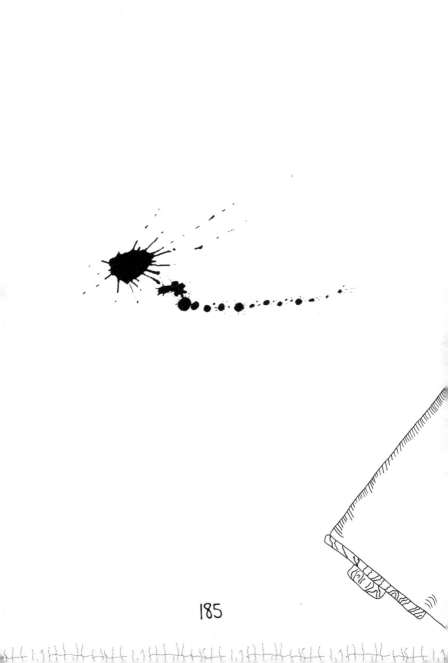

Tricky Roman Words

Dorkius wrote his diary in the year 45BC, so it probably contains some words from Roman life that you won't know. Here are some brief explanations:

Amphitheatre — A round or oval building where Romans watched gruesome things such as gladiator fights and wild-beast shows.

Atrium — The main hall of a Roman house. Unlike today's hallways, it featured an open ceiling, a small pool and no embarrassing photos of you as a baby.

Augur — To tell the future by understanding omens. The ancient Romans had all sorts of crazy theories about sacred chickens and pig innards, unlike modern, sophisticated humans who follow horoscopes.

Barbarians – The name Romans gave to everyone else. They considered foreigners to be totally uncivilized and smelly, even though they just had different languages and cultures. Although some foreigners did chew with their mouths open.

Decimation – A form of military punishment in which one soldier was selected at random and killed by nine others. So anyone who uses the word 'decimated' to mean 'totally destroyed' is wrong ... and should be totally destroyed.

Elysium – The coolest bit of the Roman afterlife. Rather like a modern VIP enclosure, except you had to be a dead hero to get in, rather than a footballer or a reality TV star.

Forum – The large market square in the middle of a Roman town where you could shop and mingle with others. You could also have pointless arguments with random strangers, which is why Internet discussion boards have the same name.

Gladiators – Ruthless fighters who were pitted against each other, sometimes to the death, in huge arenas. Gladiators were often slaves or prisoners of war, though some were eventually freed. Many of these went on to teach in gladiator schools, where they were even more ruthless than PE teachers are today.

The Ides of March – The 15th of March. This was a very important date in the history of Rome because ... well let's just say that Dorkius's mum's priest wasn't wrong about everything.

Julius Caesar – Roman leader, general, author and baldy. Caesar was made 'dictator for 10 years' shortly before Dorkius started his diary.

Mosaic – A picture made up of lots of small pieces of stone, glass or pottery.

Senate – The elected politicians of ancient Rome. Unlike today's politicians, they were scheming, ruthless and prone to violence. Sorry, that should have read 'Exactly like today's politicians, they were scheming, ruthless and prone to violence.'

Toga – The heavy woollen cloth worn by Roman citizens. People sometimes still have toga parties today, but they usually wear light cotton sheets and rarely sacrifice any animals to the gods.

Villa – A large , posh house, often centrally heated.

A Note On Roman Numerals

Ancient Romans didn't use the numerals we usually use today. They used a combination of the letters I, V, X, L, C, D and M. Roman numerals are still used on posh watches and movie sequels.

Here's a quick guide:

1 = I	11 = XI
2 = II	12 = XII
3 = III	13 = XIII
4 = IV	14 = XIV
5 = V	15 = XV
6 = VI	16 = XVI
7 = VII	17 = XVII
8 = VIII	18 = XVIII
9 = IX	19 = XIX
10 = X	20 = XX

21 = XXI	40 = XL
22 = XXII	50 = L
23 = XXIII	60 = LX
24 = XXIV	100 = C
25 = XXV	200 = CC
26 = XXVI	500 = D
27 = XXVII	1000 = M
28 = XXVIII	1500 = MD
29 = XXIX	2000 = MM
30 = XXX	2020 = MMXX

Follow Dorkius in his next hilarious adventure as he travels with Julius Caesar to ancient Egypt. Out in summer 2013.

ISBN: 978-1-78055-028-2